Cat S

Maine Coons

NICKI CLAUSEN-GRACE

BLACK RABBIT BOOKS

Bolt is published by Black Rabbit Books
P.O. Box 3263, Mankato, Minnesota, 56002.
www.blackrabbitbooks.com
Copyright © 2020 Black Rabbit Books

Jennifer Besel, editor; Catherine Cates,
interior designer; Grant Gould, cover designer;
Omay Ayres, photo researcher

Library of Congress Cataloging-in-Publication Data
Names: Clausen-Grace, Nicki, author.
Title: Maine coons / by Nicki Clausen-Grace.
Description: Mankato, Minnesota : Black Rabbit Books, [2020] |
Series: Bolt. Cat stats | Includes bibliographical references and index. |
Audience: Age 8-12. | Audience: Grade 4 to 6.
Identifiers: LCCN 2018020628 (print) | LCCN 2018021827 (ebook) |
ISBN 9781680728057 (e-book) | ISBN 9781680727999 (library binding) |
ISBN 9781644660164 (paperback)
Subjects: LCSH: Maine coon cat—Juvenile literature.
Classification: LCC SF449.M34 (ebook) | LCC SF449.M34 C53 2020 (print) |
DDC 636.8/3—dc23
LC record available at https://lccn.loc.gov/2018020628

Printed in the United States of America. 1/19

Image Credits

Getty: Brooke Pennington, 18
(t); iStock: undefined undefined,
4–5; Shutterstock: ALEKSEI SEMYKIN,
13 (t); alexavol, 17 (br); Andrea Izzotti 18
(b); Artbox, 3; Bachkova Natalia, 13 (b); CJan-
suebsri, 20–21 (bkgd all circles); DenisNata, Cover,
10, 20–21 (adolescent); DragoNika, 17 (t); Elena
Butinova, 17 (bl); Eric Isselee, 1, 22 (cat), 28, 32; Er-
molaev Alexander, 31; HannaMonika, 17 (bm); Happy
monkey, 20–21 (senior); Henk Vrieselaar, 24 (X-ray);
Kristi Blokhin, 24–25 (cat); mholka, 23 (b); MyImages
- Micha, 14 (toy), 22 (toy); nuclear_lily, 14 (top cat);
Okeanasm 14 (b); otsphoto, 20; Seregraff,
8–9, 20 (adult); Sergey Ginak,
6; V.Borisov, 23 (t); ViChizh, 26–27
Every effort has been made to contact copyright
holders for material reproduced in this
book. Any omissions will be rectified in
subsequent printings if notice is
given to the publisher.

Contents

CHAPTER 1

Meet the

A large cat sits on the counter
watching its owner wash dishes.
Suddenly the cat leans in for a drink.
The cat splashes water all over.
Its owner laughs.

Maine Coons are the official state cat of Maine.

Maine Coon History

The Maine Coons' name gives a big clue to where these cats are from. They are from the U.S. state of Maine. **Colonial** settlers found these cats when they first arrived. No one is sure how they got there. But the cats **adapted** to survive the cold Maine winters.

PARTS OF A MAINE COON

SHAGGY COAT

LONG TAIL

OVAL EYES

EAR TUFTS

LARGE PAWS

9

Maine Coons make a sound called a trill.
It's a mix of a meow and a purr.

CHAPTER 2

A Special

People often compare Maine Coons to dogs. These cats are very **loyal** to their owners. They like to spend time with their humans. They also enjoy playing fetch. And they will learn to walk on leashes.

Having Fun

Maine Coons are friendly and curious cats. Unlike most cats, Maine Coons really like to play in water. They will splash with their paws. They might jump in a sink, tub, or birdbath for a quick dip.

Early Maine Coons survived by hunting mice and birds. The cats still have that hunting **instinct**. They might bring **prey** back to their owners.

Some Maine Coons
even swim.

Maine Coons get along
well with other pets.

Popular Cat

Maine Coons are one of the most popular cats in the United States. They are smart and have plenty of energy. They enjoy games where they chase toys. But they remain gentle, even as they pretend to hunt.

Maine Coons'

Maine Coons are big cats. They are the largest **domestic** cat breed. Their bodies are built to live in cold weather. Shaggy coats **repel** water. Fluffy tails wrap around them for warmth. The cats' big feet work like snowshoes.

COMPARING SIZES

MAINE COON	RAGDOLL	AMERICAN SHORTHAIR
up to 25 POUNDS (11 kilograms)	**up to 20 POUNDS**	**up to 15 POUNDS** (7 kg)

A Coat of Many Colors

Maine Coons have long, silky coats. They come in up to 75 different color combinations. Some are solid colors. Others have **tabby** patterns. The most common is a brown tabby.

The cats can have many eye colors too. Their eyes are usually copper, green, gold, or blue. Some cats are odd-eyed. They have two different colored eyes.

Maine Coon

Life Cycle

KITTEN

Kittens learn to run, jump, and play.

Older Maine Coons move a little slower. These cats live up to 15 years.

ADOLESCENT

Maine Coons reach full size at around four to five years old.

ADULT

Adults still like to play.

SENIOR

CHAPTER 4

Caring

for a Maine Coon

Like all pets, Maine Coons need care from their owners. Their long hair needs to be combed twice a week. They also need food, water, and a clean litter box every day.

Maine Coons should play every day for exercise. Play also keeps them from getting bored.

Cat Games

chasing a toy on a string

playing with toys that look like birds or mice

fetching toys

23

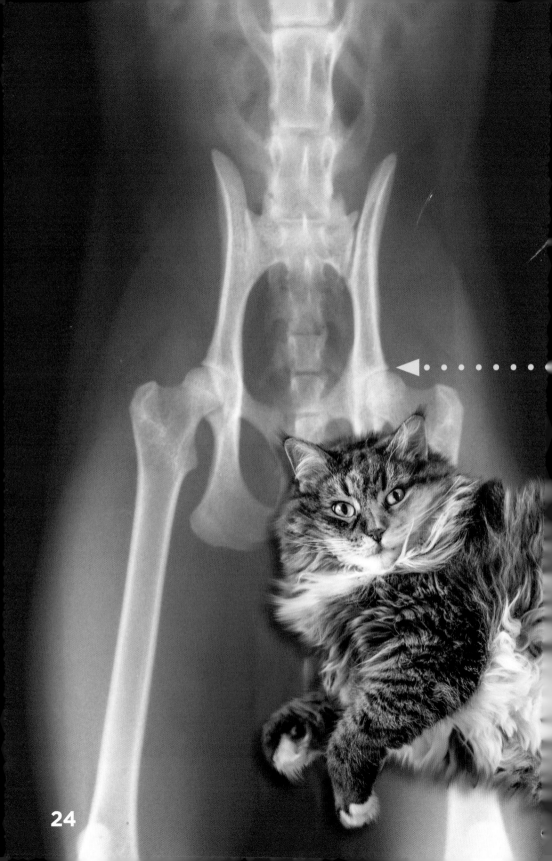

Health Concerns

Maine Coons are usually healthy. One problem to watch for is **obesity**. Owners must be careful to keep their Coons from overeating. Some Maine Coons have problems with their hips or hearts too. Getting regular vet checkups can help avoid health problems.

Friendly Family Member

With its happy trill and friendly nature, the Maine Coon makes a great pet. It's no wonder these are such popular cats. People who want a big armful of cat should look no further.

Is a Maine Coon

Right for You?

Answer the questions below.
Then add up your points to see
if a Maine Coon is a good fit.

1 **Do you want a cat that climbs up high?**

A. Yes. Watching them climb is fun.
(1 point)

B. Sometimes it's nice to have a cat
watch from above. (2 points)

C. I want my cat on the ground by me.
(3 points)

2 Do you need a cat that gets along with dogs?

A. My cat won't ever be around a dog. **(1 point)**

B. Maybe. We might get a dog one day. **(2 points)**

C. My cat needs to be friendly to my dog. **(3 points)**

3 Do you want a cat that loves water?

A. Why would my cat get wet? **(1 point)**

B. I don't mind. **(2 points)**

C. I'd love to splash around together. **(3 points)**

3 points
A Maine Coon is not your perfect match.
4-8 points
A Maine Coon might work. But there might be a better breed for you.
9 points
You and a Maine Coon would get along well!

29

adapt (uh-DAPT)—to change something so it works better or is better suited for a purpose

colonial (kuh-LOH-nee-uhl)—relating to the time of the original 13 colonies of the United States; the time lasted between 1492 and 1763.

domestic (doh-MES-tik)—tame or living near or with humans

instinct (IN-stingkt)—a natural, unplanned behavior in response to something

loyal (LOY-uhl)—having complete support for someone or something

obesity (oh-BEE-si-tee)—the condition of being very fat or overweight

prey (PRAY)—an animal hunted or killed for food

repel (ri-PEL)—to keep something out or away

tabby (TAH-bee)—a domestic cat with a striped and spotted coat

BOOKS
Felix, Rebecca. *Maine Coons.* Cool Cats. Minneapolis: Bellwether Media, 2016.

Furstinger, Nancy, and John Willis. *Maine Coon Cats.* All about Cats. New York: AV2 by Weigl, 2018.

Schuh, Mari. *Maine Coon Cats.* Favorite Cat Breeds. Mankato, MN: Amicus High Interest, 2017.

WEBSITES
Animals for Kids: Maine Coon Cat
www.ducksters.com/animals/maine_coon_cat.php

Breed Profile: The Maine Coon
cfa.org/Breeds/BreedsKthruR/MaineCoon.aspx

Maine Coon
www.animalplanet.com/tv-shows/cats-101/videos/maine-coon